THE TEDDY BEARS' PICNIC

ILLUSTRATED BY
BRUCE WHATLEY

HarperCollins*Publishers*

For Mummy Bear
—B.W.

"The Teddy Bears' Picnic"
(John W. Bratton, Jimmy Kennedy)
© 1947 Warner Bros., Inc.
Illustrations © 1996 by Bruce Whatley
Printed in China. All rights reserved. Used by permission.
ISBN 0-06-027302-X. — ISBN 0-06-443655-1 (pbk.)
Typography by Tom Starace
❖
Visit us on the World Wide Web!   http://www.harperchildrens.com

THE TEDDY BEARS' PICNIC

If you go down to the woods today
You're sure of a big surprise

If you go down to the woods today
You better go in disguise

For every bear that ever there was
Will gather there for certain because
Today's the day the teddy bears
Have their picnic.

Every teddy bear who's been good
Is sure of a treat today
There's lots of marvelous things to eat
And wonderful games to play

Beneath the trees, where nobody sees
They'll hide and seek as long as they please

Picnic time for teddy bears
The little teddy bears
Are having a lovely time today

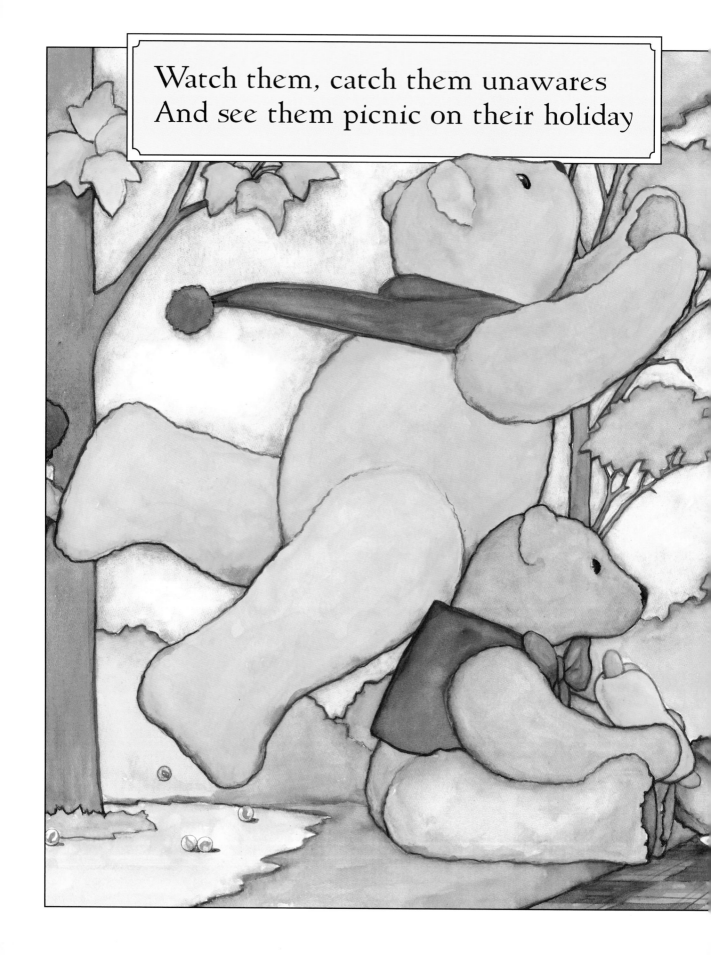

Watch them, catch them unawares
And see them picnic on their holiday

See them gaily gad about
They love to play and shout
They never have any cares

At six o'clock their mommies and daddies
Will take them home to bed
Because they're tired little teddy bears.

If you go down in the woods today
You better not go alone

It's lovely down in the woods today
But safer to stay at home

For every bear that ever there was
Will gather there together because
Today's the day the teddy bears
Have their picnic.